Pillow of Dreams

Peter Jan Honigsberg

illustrated by

Tony Morse

RDR Books

Oakland, California

One look at Margaret Bunny's special pillow makes her sleepy. She places her head down on that soft, fluffy pillow and wonderful dreams begin.

In one dream Margaret will never forget, yellow, pink and blue angel bunnies flew up to the sky. Her very own guardian angel bunny was among them.

Then there was the time Margaret dreamed of a thirsty moon dipping down to drink from a beautiful lake. The moon must have been very thirsty that night, for she didn't stop drinking until sunrise.

When Margaret's teacher reads stories to her class about far away lands, the rest of the class can only imagine what it

would be like to visit. But with her magic pillow, Margaret sees them in her dreams.

One day, when Margaret
was telling her friends
about one of her dreams,
a neighbor named
Newberry Mole overheard
her. "I need a pillow like that,"
he said to himself.

That afternoon, while
Margaret and her family were out,
Newberry Mole burrowed into the bunny house. He ran down-
stairs to Margaret's room, grabbed the pillow from her bed
and raced home.

"Now I can dream of getting the things I want," says Newberry. "The first thing I want is money. Lots of it."

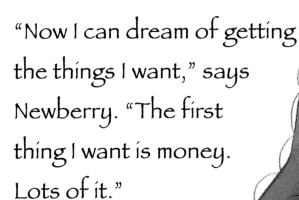

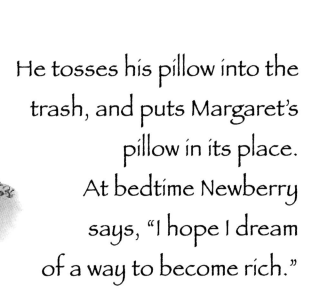

He tosses his pillow into the trash, and puts Margaret's pillow in its place. At bedtime Newberry says, "I hope I dream of a way to become rich."

Sure enough, Newberry dreams of going into a bank and snatching a big bag of money from the counter. But the police arrest him as he leaves the bank. Newberry Mole wakes from his bad dream in a cold sweat.

"Next time," he says, "I will think of another way to get rich."

That night, when the Bunny family returns home, Margaret lies down and knows right away that something is wrong. "My pillow," she cries. "Where's my pillow?"

"Maybe it fell on the floor," says mother.

But it is not there.

"Maybe it is under the bed," says her father.

But it is not there either.

Her brothers and sisters can't find the missing pillow of dreams. It is nowhere to be found.

"We all need to go to bed now," Margaret's mother says after searching and searching.

"It's very late. We will look for it again in the morning."

Margaret Bunny does not sleep very well that night. She misses her special pillow.

Meanwhile, Newberry Mole is preparing for sleep. "This time I will dream of finding a treasure," he says. "Then I will be able to keep it."

That night, Newberry dreams of finding buried gold and silver. He holds a map with an "X" marking the spot of the treasure. Then he digs and digs. When his shovel hits the treasure chest, he can not believe his eyes. The chest is filled with gold and silver coins. But he can't lift the chest because it is too heavy.

As he sits, wondering what to do, a fox strolls by. Newberry quickly closes the chest. He has an idea.

"Oh Mr. Fox," says Newberry. "Would you mind giving me a hand with this old chest? I'll give you ten gold coins if you'll help me carry it to my home."

"Sure," answers the fox. "But what is in your chest?"

"Oh, nothing special," replies Newberry, "just some old things."

On the way, they pass a den. "Do you mind if I stop for a moment to rest?" asks the fox. "This is my home."

"Fine with me," says Newberry, although he is anxious to take his treasure home.

While Newberry Mole waits, the fox goes inside. Soon, Fox comes out with one of his brothers, followed by another brother, and then another. All eight of Fox's brothers pick up the treasure and walk away with it.

"Hey wait, that's my chest," Newberry calls.

"Not anymore," says Fox.

"This bunny pillow may be magic," says Newberry when he awakens from his dream, "but it sure isn't doing me any good. Tonight, I hope I dream of living in a castle."

Sure enough, that night Newberry dreams of a beautiful castle, a castle that belongs to Mr. Beaver. But Beaver has broken his leg. He asks Newberry to take care of him.

Newberry thinks this is a wonderful idea. He hopes that Beaver will give him a big reward. So, Newberry waits on Beaver for weeks. After he recovers, Beaver says, "Thank you very much," and cooks the mole a delicious dinner. But he does not give Newberry any money.

"I've had it with this pillow," says Newberry. "It is not working for me the way it worked for Margaret." He thinks of how the little bunny is missing her special pillow. Newberry decides to return it and tell her he is very sorry.

Margaret forgives Newberry when he returns the pillow and invites him to stay for dessert. "You have made us so happy," says Margaret's mother.

Newberry, still feeling embarrassed, joins the bunny family for cake and ice cream. Margaret hugs her pillow the whole time. When Newberry rises to leave, mother bunny gives him another piece of cake to take home.

That night, Newberry decides to try something new. "My special dreams did not work out the way I planned, even with Margaret's magic pillow. I'll just go get my own worn pillow, and let my dreams be what they may."

That night, Newberry Mole dreams of visiting the land of rainbows, where the sun plays in giant waterfalls. There are circular rainbows, double rainbows, and even miniature rainbows Newberry can carry in his pocket. He has great fun running and splashing in the rainbow puddles.

There is no pot of gold at the end of any of these rainbows, but he does not seem to mind. Newberry Mole awakens with a big smile in his heart. Now he knows for sure that the only dreams worth having are the ones you can call your own.

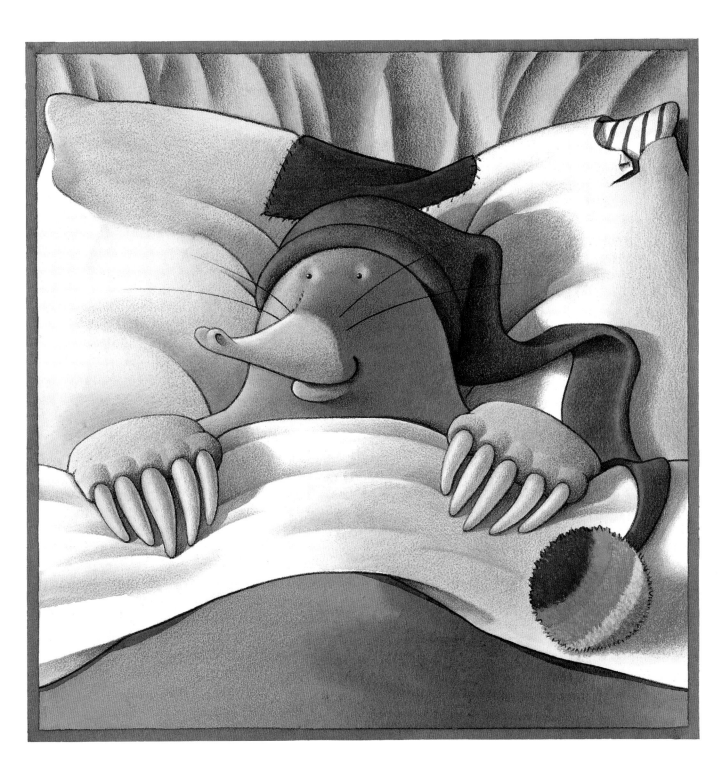

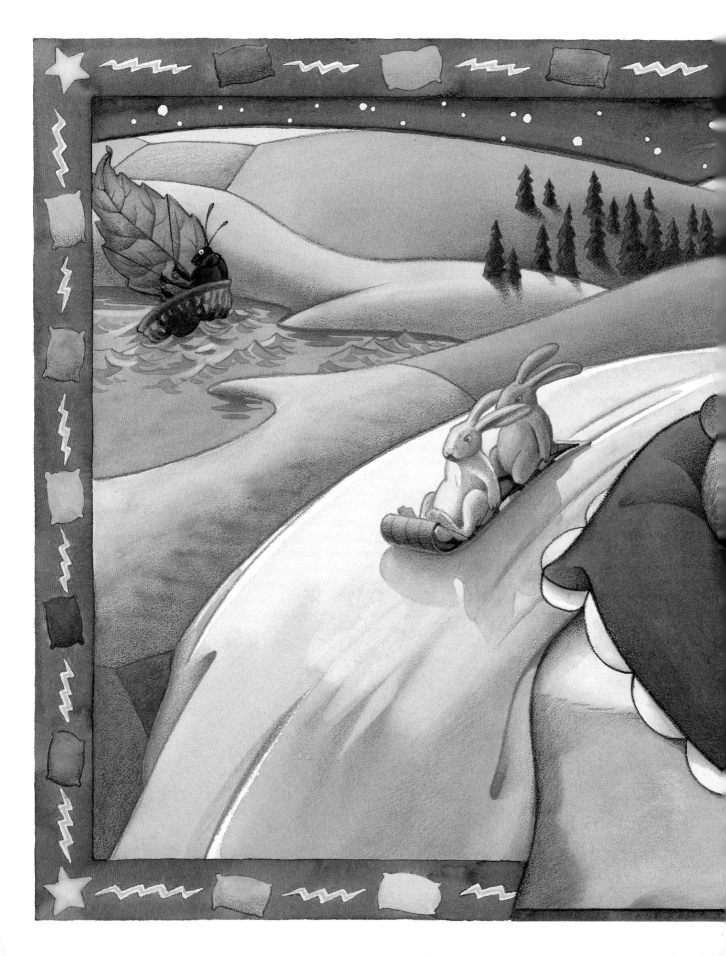

PILLOW OF DREAMS

RDR Books
4456 Piedmont Avenue
Oakland, California 94611

Library of Congress Catalog Card Number: 99-093454

ISBN 1-57143-076-8

Cover and book design: Paula Morrison

Printed in Canada